William Willis

Genealogy of the McKinstry Family

SALZWASSER
VERLAG

William Willis

Genealogy of the McKinstry Family

Reprint of the original, first published in 1858.

1st Edition 2023 | ISBN: 978-3-37515-228-4

Verlag (Publisher): Salzwasser Verlag GmbH, Zeilweg 44, 60439 Frankfurt, Deutschland
Vertretungsberechtigt (Authorized to represent): E. Roepke, Zeilweg 44, 60439 Frankfurt, Deutschland
Druck (Print): Books on Demand GmbH, In de Tarpen 42, 22848 Norderstedt, Deutschland

GENEALOGY

OF THE

McKINSTRY FAMILY,

WITH

A PRELIMINARY ESSAY

ON THE

Scotch-Irish Immigrations to America.

BY WILLIAM WILLIS,
OF PORTLAND, ME.

BOSTON:
HENRY W. DUTTON & SON, PRINTERS,
TRANSCRIPT BUILDING.
1858.

THE McKINSTRY FAMILY.

The McKinstrys originated in Scotland. The first of the name who emigrated to Ireland was Rodger, who had lived in the neighborhood of Edinburgh, and emigrated thence to the north of Ireland about the year 1669. I propose, as a preliminary to the history of this family, to give a brief account of the Scotch emigration to Ireland, and from that country to America previous to our Revolution.

During the Irish rebellions in the reign of Elizabeth, the Province of Ulster, embracing the northern counties of Ireland, was greatly depopulated, and it became a favorite project with her successor, James I., to repeople those counties with a protestant population, the better to preserve order, and introduce a higher state of cultivation in that portion of his dominions. To promote this object, liberal offers of land were made, and other inducements held out in England and Scotland, for persons to occupy this wide and vacant territory. The project was eagerly embraced; companies and colonies were formed, and individuals without organization were tempted to partake of the advantageous offers of government. A London company, among the first to enter upon this new acquisition, established itself at Derry, and gave such a character to the place as to cause it to be afterwards and forever known as the renowned city of Londonderry.

The first emigration from Scotland was chiefly from the Highlands, where agricultural resources were scanty and often wholly cut off, and where the fruits of labor were gathered from a stern soil. Sir Hugh Montgomery, the sixth Laird of Braidstone, a friend and follower of King James, was among the earliest to obtain possession of forfeited land in the county of Down, and laid his rough hand upon many broad acres. The coast of Scotland is within twenty miles of the county of Antrim in Ireland, and across this frith or strait flowed from the northeast a population distinguished for thrift, industry and endurance, which has given a peculiar and elevated character to that portion of the emerald island. It is said that the clan McDonald contributed largely to this emigration, and was among the first of the Scottish nation to plant upon its shores. They scattered chiefly in the counties of Down, Londonderry and Antrim, and greatly assisted to build up Newry, Bangor, Derry and Belfast, the principal cities of those counties.

This was the first protestant population that was introduced into Ireland, the Presbyterians of Scotland furnishing the largest element; and they have maintained their ascendancy to the present day, against the persevering efforts of the Episcopalians on the one hand, and of the Romanists, bigoted and numerous, by whom they were surrounded, on the other. The first Presbyterian church established in Ireland was in Ballycarry, in the county of Antrim, in 1613.

The Clan Alpine, otherwise called the McGregors, in the latter part of the 17th century, had made themselves very obnoxious to government and the neighboring clans by a wild and reckless course of life. Argyle, the chief of the Campbells, their inveterate enemy, who was high in court favor, procured a decree of extermination against them, extending even to the obliteration of their name and place of residence. Heavy penalties were proclaimed against all who bore the badge of the clan. To avoid this withering persecution, many sought refuge in the neighboring islands; many changed their names and fled to remote parts of their own country or to other countries. Descendants from this clan are now found in the United States and elsewhere, under the names of Grier, Greer, Gregor, Gregory, &c., the Mac being dropped. Thus we shall probably find that a distinguished Judge of the Supreme Court of the U. States, residing in Pennsylvania, Judge Grier, derives his origin from the same wild tribe, which, under the guidance of Robroy McGregor, was the terror of the high and low lands of his native soil. Nor was the change of name confined to that clan; for we are assured that the Mackinnons, from the isle of Skye, are now McKenna, McKean, McCannon; that McNish has become McNiece, Meness, Munniss, and Moniss; and Graham is Graeme, Grimes, Groom, &c.

Although the rebellions of 1715 and 1745, against the House of Hanover, made large additions to the Scotch population in the north of Ireland, yet by far the largest accessions to this colonization were occasioned by religious persecutions in the time of the latter Stuarts. That fated race, blind to the dictates of justice and humanity, and devoted with sullen bigotry to their peculiar notions in religion and politics, pursued a system of measures best calculated to wean from their support subjects the most devoted to their cause. The Scottish race was bound to the Stuarts by a national prejudice and a sincere affection. But they were imbued with a religious enthusiasm, inspired by Knox their great apostle, which ruled their consciences, and rendered the sanctions of a higher law superior to their patriotism, or their attachment to their native sovereigns. Rather, they believed that true patriotism consisted in maintaining the religion transmitted by their fathers.

When, therefore, the Charleses and James II. endeavored to introduce prelacy among them, and to force it upon their consciences by arbitrary laws and the iron hoofs of the dragoons of Claverhouse, very many of these hardy, persistent and enduring Presbyterians, having suffered to the bitter end of cruelty and oppression, abandoned the land of their birth, the home of their fondest affections, and sought an asylum among their countrymen in the secure retreats of Ulster, or fled across the ocean. They carried their household gods with them; and their religious peculiarities became more dear in their land of exile, for the dangers and sorrows through which they had borne them.

Presbyterianism was transported from Geneva to Scotland by John Knox, who composed his first Book of Discipline, containing the substance of his intended policy, in 1561. In 1566, a general assembly approved the Discipline; and all church affairs, after that time, were managed by Presbyteries and General Assemblies. They did not at first formally deprive the bishops, who had ecclesiastical jurisdiction, of their power, but they went on gradually and steadily doing it, as they acquired confidence and strength. In 1574, they voted bishops to be only pastors of one parish; in 1577, they decreed that bishops should be called by their own names without title; and the next year they declared the name of bishop to be a nuisance. In 1580, they pronounced with one voice, in the General Assembly, that diocesan episcopacy was unscriptural and unlawful. The same year, King James and his family, with the whole Scotch nation, subscribed a confession of faith, embracing the "solemn league and covenant," obliging them to maintain the protestant doctrine and presbyterian government. Thus, in the space of twenty years, grew up this formal, extensive and powerful institution, twining itself over the Scottish mind with stern and inflexible bands, which death only could sunder; and for which, home, country, life—all things beside—were freely given up.

James had hardly become secure and easy on his English throne when he began his attack upon the religious system of his early life, and of his native country, and his successors followed it up with a pertinacity worthy of a better cause. The attempts to establish the church of England over Scotland, and destroy the religious system so universally established and so dearly cherished by that devoted people, was pursued by the Charleses and James the 2d, by persecutions as mean, as cruel, and savage, as any which have disgraced the annals of religious bigotry and crime. And they did not cease until they had greatly depopulated Scotland, and were stripped of their power by the happy revolution under William and Mary, which restored repose to a distracted and long suffering people.

Scotland, a country no larger than Maine, with a population at the close of the seventeenth century of a million, and in 1800 not so much as the present population of Massachusetts and Maine; with agricultural and other resources by no means equal to ours—of which a writer in a recent number of the Edinburgh Review, on the Highlands, says, " at the end of the 17th century the chief social feature of the Highlands was famine, and another was emigration." Yet this country has contributed largely, by emigration, to furnish numerous and prominent settlers for many other lands; to the nation with which she is connected, profound statesmen, brilliant writers, and men the most renowned in every department of scientific and philosophical research.

This is the race, composed of various tribes flowing from different parts of Scotland, which furnished the materials of the Scotch-Irish immigration to this country. By their industry, frugality and skill, they had made the deserted region into which they had moved a comparatively rich and flourishing country. They had improved agriculture and introduced manufactures, and by the excellence and high reputation of their productions had attracted trade and commerce to their markets, so as to excite the jealousy of government in the reigns of Anne and the first George, notwithstanding that by their efforts and example the prosperity of the whole island had been promoted. The patronizing government began to recognize them, in the shape of taxes and embarrassing regulations upon their industry and trade. The same jealousy controlled that government afterwards, in regard to the American Colonies, by which the commerce and enterprise of their subjects on this side of the ocean, were, in like manner, hampered and restricted, so that they were hardly permitted to manufacture articles of the most common necessity, but were driven to import them from the mother country, as glass, nails, hats, cloths, &c.

These restrictions occasioned general distress, not only in the north of Ireland, but throughout the whole island. To this, Douglass (p. 368) says, " was added an extravagant advance in rents by landlords, whose long leases were now expired." The energetic and self-willed population of the north of Ireland, animated by the same spirit which subsequently moved the American mind, determined no longer to endure these oppressive measures; and they sought by another change to find a freer verge for the exercise of their industry and skill, and for the enjoyment of their religion.

One of their spiritual leaders, the Rev. Mr. McGregor, in a sermon which he preached on the eve of the departure from Ireland, assigned the following reasons for their removal to America: 1, to avoid oppressive and cruel bondage; 2, to shun persecution; 3, to withdraw from the communion of idolaters; 4, to have an opportunity of worshipping God according to the dictates of conscience and his inspired word. He looked at it chiefly from a religious point of view; others, from a material and commercial stand point. It was undoubtedly suggested and promoted by a variety of motives gradually operating upon the mass of the population, which brought them to the determination, solemn and painful, to sunder the ties which had bound them firmly to their adopted country, and impelled them to seek new and doubtful homes in a wild, unexplored, and far-distant land.

The first immigration of these people to this country was to the Middle and Southern Colonies. As early as 1684 a settlement was formed in New Jersey, and in 1690 small groups were found in the Carolinas, Maryland and Pennsylvania. But it was not until the reigns of Anne and George I. that large numbers, driven by oppressive measures of government and disastrous seasons, were induced to seek, even in the wilderness, a better home than their old settled region could give them. Gordon says, "Scarcity of corn, generally prevalent from the discouragement of industry, amounted in 1728 and the following year almost to a famine, especially in Ulster. Emigrations to America, which have since increased, drew above 3000 people annually from Ulster alone." Dr. Boulter, afterwards Archbishop of Armagh, who labored strenuously in 1728 to divert the horrors of famine in Ireland, wrote to the English ministry, March 7, 1728, that there were seven ships then lying at Belfast that " are carrying off about 1000 passengers; most of them can neither get victuals nor work at home." He also says, "3100 men, women and children went from Ireland to America in 1727, and 4200 in three years, all protestants." The principal seats of these emigrations were Pennsylvania and the Middle States. New England was found not so favorable to their farming and other interests. Douglass, who wrote at Boston in 1750, says, "at first they chose New England, but being brought up to husbandry, &c., New England did not answer so well as the Colonies southward; at present they generally resort to Pennsylvania." By Proud's history of Pennsylvania, we find that in 1729 near 6000 arrived in that Colony; and before the middle of the century nearly 12,000 arrived annually for several years. These were protestants and generally Presbyterians; few or no Catholics came, until some time after the Revolution.

In the summer of 1718, the first organized company of this class of immigrants, of which we have any knowledge, left the shores of Ireland in five vessels, containing 120 families, for the new world, and arrived safely in Boston, August 4, 1718. Here all was new, the wilderness and the world before them. Imagine this little colony, strangers in a strange land, seeking new homes and not knowing whither to turn. There they lie at the little wharf at the foot of State Street in the town of Boston, which then contained about 12,000 inhabitants, taking counsel where to go, and how to dispose of themselves and their little ones, to begin the world anew. With their wonted energy, they were soon astir. One brigantine, with a company of twenty families, sought their fortunes at the eastward, among whom were Armstrong, Means, McKean, Gregg;—they spent a hard and long winter in Portland harbor, and then fled westward, most of them, to join their companions in founding their new Londonderry. Another portion went to Andover and its neighborhood, led on by their pastor McGregor; another to Pelham, Mass., under the lead of the Rev. Mr. Abercrombie; another remained in Boston, under their pastor the Rev. John Moorhead ; and still another sought refuge in Worcester and its vicinity. Wherever they went, this devoted people first of all planted the Presbyterian church, adopting the discipline and usages of the church of Scotland. Mr. McGregor and his flock finally established themselves at Nutfield, in N. H., and built up a town which they called, from their venerated city in Ireland, Londonderry. Here they founded a colony, which, like a fruitful mother, has been sending forth from its prolific bosom men and women, of their hardy and enlightened stock, to instruct and adorn society. And here were gathered the McGregors, McClintocks, Starks, Reid, Bell, Morrison, Anderson, McKean, and others, who have given vigor to our varied institutions.

The society in Boston established the Presbyterian church, which continued for more than half a century to worship in their meeting-house on the corner of Long Lane and Bury Street, where Dr. Gannett's church now stands, under the pastoral care of Rev. John Moorhead, familiarly called Johnny Moorhead, whose ardent and impulsive temper often led him into embarrassments, but who faithfully ministered to his people until his death in 1773. He was succeeded by the Rev. Robert Annan, a Scotch presbyter, who occupied the pulpit until 1786, when the people cast off Presbyterianism, assumed the Congregational form of government, and, in 1787, settled the excellent and learned Dr. Jeremy Belknap. In 1745, they established the first Presbytery, consisting of twelve churches, called the Presbytery of Boston.

This company introduced into Boston the cultivation of the potato, which had not before been known in the country, and the flax spinning wheel, the familiar domestic instrument of their native households. The latter had quite a run in Boston ; schools were established to teach the art of spinning, and ladies of the first quality were found among the votaries of this useful art.

The party which went to Worcester fared worse than any other ; they encountered a severe persecution, and were not permitted to erect a house of worship of their peculiar order. In one attempt of the kind, the structure was entirely demolished by a mob. A great prejudice was enlisted against them, both from their religion and their country ; they were called *Irish*, a term they greatly resented. Mr. McGregor wrote, " We are surprised to hear ourselves termed Irish people." The Worcester immigrants struggled awhile against a bitter opposition, and finding repose there hopeless, they abandoned the place, some for Pelham, others for their head-quarters in Londonderry, and some to plant themselves at Unadilla, on the banks of the Susquehanna in New York. In the Worcester company were the names of Clark, McKinstry, Gray, Ferguson, Crawford, Graham, Barbour, Blair, and Thornton ; Mathew, then a child, became the distinguished patriot and statesman of New Hampshire, and a signer of the declaration of Independence.

In 1719 and 1720, five ships, under the conduct of Capt. Robert Temple, who had previously explored the country, landed several hundred families from Ireland on the shores of Kennebec River and Merry Meeting Bay. Temple was of a distinguished family in Ireland, and the ancestor of the numerous and respected family of the late Lt. Governor Thomas L. Winthrop of Boston, who married his grand-daughter Elizabeth Bowdoin.

Dummer's Indian war broke up this colony, and the larger part of them went to Pennsylvania. After the war was ended, other companies of this race occupied various points in Maine, as Topsham, Brunswick, Boothbay, Pemaquid, and the Waldo patent, which region contained a larger number of this description of immigrants than any part of New England. They were entirely under the religious government of Presbyters and Assemblies, until the eve of the Revolution, when large accessions of Congregationalists or Independents mingling among them, a struggle took place between the two orders for the government of the church. This resulted in the overthrow of Presbyterianism and the establishment of Congregationalism over the churches of the State. There is not now a Presbyterian church in Maine. Once it boasted of Murray, famed for his eloquence,—of Rutherford, Blair, Boyd, Dunlap, McLean, Urquahart, Whittaker, Strickland,—none remain, and hardly a record of them. The same struggle took place in Massachusetts, until Synod, Presbytery and Church disappeared, and now only the feeble Presbytery of Londonderry remains in New England to record and perpetuate the religious characteristics of that great race which sought refuge on these shores, and has done so much to advance the honor and prosperity of the country. Their power as a sect is most prevalent in the Middle States.

Independency or Congregationalism was not introduced into England until 1616. But Puritanism, which embraces both orders of dissenters, had its origin in Elizabeth's time, in her attempts to cause subscriptions to be made to the liturgy, ceremonies, and discipline of the Church, in 1564. Those who refused subscription and preferred a simple worship, were called Puritans by way of reproach. When the doctrines of Arminius began to prevail in the English church, the Puritans adhered to the system of Calvin, and were defined to be men of severe morals, Calvinists in doctrine, and non-conformists to the ceremonies and discipline of the Church. The first Presbyterian church was established in England, near London, in 1577, by a few scattered brethren; and both these branches of dissenters, Independents and Presbyterians, made at first but slow progress; and although agreeing in doctrine, they differed from each other on the form of government as widely as they both did from Episcopacy.

The Independents or Congregational brethren were small in number in the Westminster Assembly, although they increased prodigiously afterwards under Cromwell. They made a bold stand against the proceedings of the high Presbyterians. They maintained " that every particular congregation of Christians" has an entire and complete power of jurisdiction over its members, to be exercised by the elders thereof within itself." They add, " this they are sure must have been the form of government in the primitive church."—*Neal*, 3, 157.

The system of the Independents was attacked by the rigid Presbyterians with great severity, " as tending to break the uniformity of the church, under the pretence of liberty of conscience." But one of their number, Mr. Herle, the prolocutor of the Assembly, with great candor and good sense, remarked, " The difference between us and our brethren who are for Independency, is nothing so great as some may conceive ; at most, it does but ruffle the fringe, not any way rend the garment of Christ."

Yet the quarrel continued and has continued with more or less violence to the present day ; the sound of the controversy, even in this country, is now ringing in our ears ; in the last century it was discordant and harsh throughout our churches in the ambitious struggle for power. The controversy then related to church government, for in doctrine there was a substantial agreement. The Savoy confession of 1658 proceeds upon the plan of the Westminster Assembly ; the preface declares, " that they fully consent to the Westminster confession, for the substance of it." The disagreement was not in matters of faith, but only in matters of form.

It is not my intention to trace further the migrations of these people upon this continent. Having accompanied the earliest colony to Massachusetts, which contained the first of the McKinstry family who came to America, I leave the nation to follow the fortunes of the individual.

I. JOHN McKINSTRY, the first of the name who came to this country, was born in Brode Parish, in the county of Antrim, Ireland, in 1677. He was of Scotch descent, and was the son of Rodger McKinstry and Mary Wilson, who lived in the neighborhood of Edinburgh, until compelled by the persecutions under Charles II., about 1669, to seek security and repose with their Presbyterian brethren in the province of Ulster, and the county of Antrim. Their son John was educated at the University of Edinburgh, from which he graduated Master of Arts in 1712. It may gratify the curious to see the Diploma which that University then granted to its graduates, which we annex in the original language :—

" Ne quem forte habeat cujus scire interest, Nos Universitatis—Jacobi Regis Edinensis Professores Testamur hunc Juvenem Johannem McKinstrie Hibernum, Post quam Philosophiæ & Humanioribus Literis ea Morum Integritate et Modestia (quæ Ingenuum decebat Adolescentem) apud. Nos vacasset, eaque præstitisset, omnia quæ Disciplinæ Ratio et Academiæ consuetudo praescripserat ; Tandem consensu Senatus Academici Magistrum in Artibus Liberalibus Riti Renunciatum, Cunctaque consecutum Privelegia quæ Bonarum Artium Magistris uspiam concedi solent: Cujus Rei quo major esset fides, Sigillum Inclyti Senatores Edinensis Athenæi Curatores et Patroni Nos Chirographa Apposuimus IV. Kal. Martii MDCCXII. Datum Edinburgi.

JOH. GOODALL,   L. S. P.
ROBERTUS HENDERSON B & Acad. ab Archivi.
GULIEL. HAMILTON, N. S. P.
GULIELMUS LAW,   P. P.
GULIELMUS SCOT,   P. P.
ROBERTUS STOUAOL,   P. P.
COL: DRUMOND,   P. P.
JA: GREGORY,   Math. P."

Translation.—"Be it known to all whom it may concern, that we, the Professors of the University of Edinboro' of King James, testify, that this youth, John McKinstry of Ireland, after having completed the study of philosophy and human literature with the integrity and modesty of manners which is becoming an ingenuous youth, has graduated with us, and is entitled to all the privileges which the course of discipline and the custom of this Academy is accustomed to confer. And now, with the consent of the Faculty and teachers of this College, he is declared a Master in the liberal Arts, and entitled to all the privileges which are wont to be conceded to the Masters of the Good Arts. Of which fact, that there may be greater faith, we, the distinguished Governors, Teachers and Patrons of the University of Edinburgh, have placed our signatures, this 4th Calends of March, 1712."

How he disposed of himself for the next six years we have no information; he certainly qualified himself for the ministry, and undoubtedly received Presbyterian ordination. He joined the company of emigrants from the north of Ireland in the summer of 1718, and arrived in Boston, August 4, 1718. He followed the fortunes of that portion of the immigrants which went to Worcester County. He had not long been there before his services were sought by the people of Sutton, a new town near Worcester, the settlement of which had just commenced. At a meeting of the inhabitants, Nov. 25, 1719, it was voted that Mr. McKinstry should preach three months, and have fifteen pounds for the service. In the following March, the town voted to settle Mr. McKinstry, and to pay him £60 a year salary. In pursuance of this and other votes, he was duly settled according to Congregational usage on the 9th of November, 1720. The people were generally Congregationalists, while the pastor, born and educated in rigid Presbyterianism, could not, in his new position, lay aside his attachments to the religious usages of his life. Difficulties therefore arose soon after his settlement, on these opposite views of church government, which produced continued uneasiness in the parish, and led to a separation in September, 1728. Mr. McKinstry concluded to join his brethren of the same denomination in New York. On his way thither, his wife's health failing, he rested at East Windsor in Connecticut. The parish in the eastern precinct of the town, afterwards called Ellington, having no preacher, he was requested to supply the pulpit. This circumstance resulted in a suspension of his journey southward, and a settlement over that parish, as its first pastor, in 1733. He continued in this situation sixteen years, and remained in the town until his death, which took place on Sunday, January 20, 1754, at the age of 77 years. He preached on the Sunday previous to his death. Mr. McKinstry is said to have been a gentleman of good abilities, of popular talents, and unwavering integrity, a quality belonging to the family. His wife died Oct. 25, 1762, aged 81.

Soon after his settlement in Sutton, he married Elizabeth Fairfield, of Wenham, Mass., probably a daughter of William Fairfield, who represented his town in the General Court twenty-seven years, in nine of which he was Speaker of the House. By her he had seven children, viz. :—JOHN, b. Dec. 31, 1723 ; MARY, b. Jan. 24, 1726 ; ALEXANDER, b. May 16, 1729 ; WILLIAM, b. Oct. 8, 1732 ; PAUL, b. Sept. 18, 1734 ; ELIZABETH, b. May 27, 1736 ; ABIGAIL, b. March 26, 1739 : all at Ellington but the first two.

Elizabeth and Abigail died unmarried, the latter in Ellington, in April, 1814. Elizabeth was killed by a negro servant of her brother William, June 4, 1763, while she was visiting him in Taunton. The negro was fond of Elizabeth, but had been made to believe that he could obtain his freedom by killing some one of the family. He therefore took an opportunity, when his victim's back was towards him, and struck her a fatal blow on the back of her head with a flat-iron. Much excitement was produced in that quiet village and throughout the county by this sad event ; and a great crowd attended upon his trial and execution, which soon after followed.

The other five children were married and left issue, as we proceed to describe :—

II. JOHN, eldest son of Rev. John of Ellington, born in Sutton, December 31, 1723; was graduated at Yale College in 1746; was a classmate and chum of Ezra Stiles, afterwards the distinguished President of the College. Students at that time were placed on the catalogue according to the rank of their parents ; McKinstry was placed fourth in a class of twelve ; he survived all his classmates by fifteen years, and died Nov. 9, 1813, at the age of 90. He was ordained the first pastor of the 2nd Church in Springfield, now Chicopee, Mass., in 1752 ; the church was formed in September of the same year. He continued the active pastor of the Church and Society until 1789, when he was released from preaching, but discharged other duties of the pastorate until his death.

His salary for the first ten years was £45 lawful money ; this was raised to £62 and fire wood, and " a load of pine knots yearly to study by." After being relieved from preaching, his salary was reduced to £18. In 1760, he married Eunice Smith of Suffield, Conn., who died Sept. 20, 1820. They had seven children, viz.: JOHN ALEXANDER, b. 1760; EUNICE THEODOSIA, b. 1762 ; ELIZABETH LUCY, b. 1765 ; ARCHIBALD, b. 1767 ; ROGER AUGUSTUS, b. 1769 ; PERSEUS, b. 1772 ; CANDACE, b. 1774. The latter, and only survivor, is living unmarried in Chicopee. (1858.) The other children died without issue, except Roger Augustus, and Perseus, at Chicopee, as follows, viz :—

JOHN ALEXANDER,[2] April, 1840. *born Nov. 15. 1760*
EUNICE T.,[2] Feb. 1844. *.. Dec 20 1762*
ELIZABETH L.,[2] May 19, 1826. *" May 23 1765*
ARCHIBALD,[2] Sept. 11, 1800. He was a physician. *b. Sept. 14 1767*

III. ROGER AUGUSTUS, son of John[2] of Chicopee, was a tanner and currier, first in Ashfield, then in Plainfield, Mass. About 1825, he moved to Geneva, in Ohio, where he died in 1843. His wife was Chloe Elmer of Ashfield, by whom he had six children, viz :

IV. [1] AUGUSTUS, unmarried.

IV. [2] ORIN, married Marcia Cook, and died without issue, Oct. 1847.

IV. [3] EUNICE, married Nahum Daniels, and died without issue, soon after.

IV. [4] LUCINA, married the same Daniels, and is living with two children. Her husband was drowned at Erie, Penns., in 1842.

IV. [5] ARCHIBALD, lives in Geneva, Ohio. He married Mary Silver Thorn, and has children.

IV. [6] LYMAN, died young, without issue.

III. PERSEUS, sixth child of the Rev. John[2] of Chicopee, b. 1772 ; died August 23, 1829 ; was a tanner, first in Plainfield, then a farmer in Chicopee. He married Grace Williams, Oct. 24, 1803, and had eleven children, as follows, viz :

IV. [1] ELIZA, b. Sept. 25, 1804 ; living unmarried on the homestead in Chicopee, in 1857.

April IV. [2] EMILY, b. ~~August~~ 8, 1806 ; married Titus Chapin, a farmer in Chicopee, and died in 1842, leaving five children, viz : Titus,[2] Roxana,[2] Emily,[2] Lucy,[2] and Eleonora.[2]

IV. [3] THEODOSIA, b. Aug. 23, 1807 ; married Whitman Chapin, a farmer, in Chicopee, and had two children, viz : Moses Whitman,[2] and Edward.[2] Moses Whitman married Augusta Chapin of West Springfield, and has children. Theodosia is living, a widow, (1857) in Chicopee.

IV. [4] WILLIAM, b. June 8, 1809 ; died Feb. 24, 1845. He was a farmer in Chicopee; married Mary J. Frink and had two children, viz: Laura Jane[3] and Arthur.[3] The widow lives in western New York with her daughter; the son lives in Fredonia, N. Y.

IV. [5] JOHN ALEXANDER, b. April 9, 1811; he graduated at Amherst Col. in 1838; studied his profession at the East Windsor Seminary; settled as a Cong. minister in Torrington, Conn., in 1842; dismissed and settled at Harwinton, Conn., in 1857. In 1843, he married Mary E. Morton, of Hatfield, Mass., and has two children, viz: John Morton,[3] b. 1845, and William Alexander,[3] b. 1849.

IV. [6] WILLARD, b. April 9, 1813, and died an infant.

IV. [7] WILLARD, b. May 9, 1815, publisher of the Fredonia Censor, in Chatauque Co., N. Y.; married in 1843 Maria A. Durlin, and has three children, (1857) viz: Louis,[3] Willard,[5] and Anna.[6]

IV. [8] MARY, b. Nov. 2, 1817: married John Frink of South Hampton, Mass., and has five children.

IV. [9] Alfred, b. May 17, 1821; d. 1823.

IV. [10] Alfred Lyman, b. April 20, 1823; married Jane Granger, and has one son, Alfred.[3] He lives on the old homestead at Chicopee.

IV. [11] ARCHIBALD WINTHROP, b. March 19, 1828; lives at Fredonia, N. Y., and is associated with his brother Willard in the publication of the "Fredonia Censor." Sept. 3, 1857, he married Helen E., daughter of N. B. Putnam of Fredonia.

II. MARY, the second child of Rev. John[1] of Ellington, b. Jan. 24, 1726; married Daniel Ellsworth of Ellington, and had children. DANIEL,[2] b. 1753, d. Nov. 27, 1755; MINDWELL,[3] b. 1760, and d. without issue, Feb. 7, 1784; ALICE,[3] d. unmarried May 7, 1786, aged 21; ELIZABETH,[3] died June 21, 1786, aged 22; JERUSHA,[3] b. 1768, married William Morgan, and died April 29, 1820. They had four children, William,[4] and Mary,[4] who died in childhood, and two other daughters. _l '_ ?

II. ALEXANDER, the third child of Rev. John[1] of Ellington, b. May 16, 1728, and died there Nov. 9, 1759. He married Sarah Lee of Litchfield, Conn., and had three children, of whom EZEKIEL alone survived infancy. *She died Jan. 23 1758*

III. EZEKIEL, the only son of Alexander McKinstry,[2] who came to maturity, was born in Ellington, Aug. 17, 1753, and continued to reside there, a farmer, until his death, Nov. 25, 1803. He married Rosina Chapman, June 26, 1776. His widow, born Feb. 10, 1758, died April 24, 1839, aged 81. They had twelve children, viz:

IV. [1] Sarah, b. Nov. 8, 1777; married ———— Ross, and died Sept. 18, 1829.

IV. [2] Elizabeth, b. July 16, 1779; d. March, 1794.

IV. [3] Anna, b. March 5, 1781; d. Dec. 6, 1798.

IV. [4] Rosina, b. Jan. 25, 1783; married ———— Dunton, a tailor, who died in Rome, N. Y. She had two daughters, also dead; she died Sept. 1838.

IV. [5] Alexander, b. April 9, 1785; he established himself in Augusta, Georgia, as a merchant, where he married Elizabeth, daughter of Jesse Thompson of that neighborhood, by whom he had one son, Alexander, living in Mobile, Ala., 1857, a judge of the municipal court of that city; and one daughter, Ann, unmarried. Alexander,[4] died at Charleston, S. C., Nov. 6, 1823, aged 39. His widow married Dr. Henry Sullivan Lee, of Boston, son of Dr. Samuel Parsons Lee, of New York. They have had eight children, five sons and three daughters.

IV. [6] JOHN, b. June 16, 1787; died at Ellington, April 25, 1839, leaving a widow and one son, Alexander,[5] living on the old homestead.

IV. [7] FANNY, b. April 6, 1789; d. unmarried Jan. 27, 1809.

IV. [8] OLIVER, b. July 14, 1791; was a physician in Monson, Mass., where he died in March, 1852, the last survivor of Ezekiel's children. He left a family in that town.

IV. [9] LEE, b. March 8, 1793; d. May 29, 1808. *Augustus C.*

IV. [10] ELIZABETH, b. May 26, 1795. She married ———— Pease, a merchant, in Hartford, Conn., and d. July 26, 1834.

IV. [11] Jerusha, b. Jan. 8, 1798; d. Sept. 13, 18*0*.

IV. [12] Anna, b. Aug. 16, 1800; married *Wm. L.* Johnson, a lawyer, in Rome, N. Y., where she died Jan. 28, 1837. *leaving 3 daught. & 2 sons.*

II. WILLIAM, the third son and fourth child of John of Ellington, was born Oct. 8, 1732. He was a physician, and settled in Taunton, Mass. On Nov. 27, 1760, he married Priscilla, daughter of the Rev. Nathaniel Leonard, pastor of the 1st Church in Plymouth, Mass., and Priscilla, daughter of Dr. Nathaniel Rogers and Sarah Appleton of Ipswich. By her he had ten children, viz: [1] WILLIAM, b. Nov. 13, 1762; he graduated at Oxford University, Eng.; became Rector of East Grinstead and Lingfield, near London; was tutor to children of several noblemen, whom he accompanied in their travels on the continent. He was a good scholar and a polished gentleman, and died on a visit to this country, unmarried, in August, 1823. [2] PRISCILLA, b. Aug. 25, 1765; married John Hazen of New Brunswick, and had a large family. [3] SARAH, b. Aug. 14, 1767; married Major Caleb Stark, son of Gen. John Stark, and had a numerous family. [4] JOHN, b. March 6, 1769, a merchant in Boston several years; died unmarried Oct. 29, 1825. ⁵ MARY and ⁶ THOMAS, twins, b. Aug. 17, 1770. Thomas d. unmarried in 1796. Mary, married Benjamin Willis of Haverhill, Portland and Boston, Jan. 9, 1791, and had eight children. ⁷ ELIZABETH, b. Oct. 26, 1772; married to Samuel Sparhawk of Portsmouth and Concord, N. H., Secretary of that State, in 1803, by whom she had several children. ⁸ DAVID, b. 1775, and d. unmarried in New York, a merchant, in March, 1802.

They had two other children, viz: William, born and died Nov. 13, 1761; and John, who died Dec. 21, 1768, in the fifth year of his age. All in Taunton.

Dr. McKinstry had a successful business in Taunton, in 1774, although he had a feeble constitution and a consumptive habit. The Rev. Mr. Emery, in his "Ministry of Taunton," says of Dr. McKinstry, " He was a person of highly respectable personal and professional character." At that time a Capt. Gilbert, suspected of tory principles, was seized and so roughly handled by the "sons of liberty," that it became necessary to have a surgeon to dress his wounds. He protested against having a rebel doctor, but was willing that Dr. McKinstry should attend him. This suggestion excited suspicions against this amiable and popular physician. He became the subject of offensive remark, and was exposed to insult and injury. Being in feeble health and of a sensitive nature, which could not bear hard usage nor a suspected position, he thought it advisable to retire for a time to Boston. His family, which was left in Taunton, was now subject to increased annoyance. His wife, a finely educated and high spirited woman, of elegant manners, was compelled, by a large collection of females, to march around the liberty pole. She was niece of the Hon. George Leonard of Norton, and cousin of Daniel Leonard, a refugee, and afterwards chief justice of Bermuda.

This last act of insult decided the question with the family, who, not being able to enjoy repose upon their native soil, were forced to become loyalists in self defence, and they immediately joined the husband and father in Boston. So high was Dr. McKinstry's reputation in his profession, that he received from Gen. Gage the appointment of surgeon general of the hospitals in Boston.

It so happened that on the memorable 17th of June, 1775, a dinner party took place at Dr. McKinstry's house, for which invitations had been given out the day before. The dinner proved to be a solemn and silent one, and was partaken standing. Several officers were present who had been detailed to proceed with detachments of the British army to dislodge the rebels from Bunker Hill. They hastily dined and proceeded to join their corps; among them was Major John Small, a friend of the family, whose name is identified with that momentous battle. Dr. McKinstry's house stood on Hanover Street, near where the Shawmut House now is, and the children went to the top of the house to witness the cannonade.

Sarah, one of them, little dreamed that, in after-years, she would become the wife of a gallant stripling of 16, who was then fighting in the opposing ranks, by the side of his veteran father, the renowned John Stark. Twelve years after, she was wedded to that gallant soldier, Caleb Stark. Another daughter, Mary, might also have been a distant witness to the flight from the flames of Charlestown of her future husband, Benjamin Willis, a native of that devoted town, who, with his mother, was compelled to make a hasty retreat, without a backward look to their perishing property.

When Boston was evacuated, Dr. McKinstry and his family went on board the fleet, which lay ten days in Nantasket Roads waiting orders. During that time, viz., March 21, 1776, Dr. McKinstry died of consumption, on board the Dutton hospital ship, and his remains lie buried on George's Island, in that harbor.

The surviving members of the family were taken in the fleet to Halifax, and were on board the same ship with lady Howe, wife of the Admiral, where they were treated with that sympathy and kindness their unhappy condition required. The fleet took away about one thousand refugees. The family remained in Halifax, with the exception of William, the eldest son, until 1778, when they returned to the States, making Newport, R. I., their place of residence, during its occupation by the British. After its evacuation, they proceeded to Haverhill, in Mass., where a sister of Mrs. McKinstry, the wife of John White, Esq., lived; and she died there, May 26, 1786, honored and loved.

The four sons of Dr. McKinstry died unmarried, and consequently the *name* in this branch is extinct.

. Rev. WILLIAM,[2] died at Concord, N. H., August 28, 1823, aged 61.

JOHN,[2] died in Ohio, Oct. 29, 1825, aged 56.

THOMAS,[2] died at sea, 1796, aged 26, the vessel never heard from.

DAVID,[2] died in New York, in March, 1809, of consumption, aged 27.

III. The Rev. WILLIAM McKINSTRY,[2] son of Dr. William,[2] entered the naval service of Great Britain at the commencement of the revolution. In an engagement with an American privateer, in 1776, he lost his right hand and was shot overboard. He contrived to keep himself above water until the battle was over, when he was relieved from his critical situation. This changed the current of his life, and instead of becoming a naval officer, he became an episcopal clergyman, a cultivated scholar, and a gentleman of refined manners. He happened to be on the continent, and at a hotel in Munich, when Gen. Moreau arrived at the same hotel, in a most unpretending style, to take charge of the French army in that neighborhood. In a few days after was fought the celebrated battle of Hohenlinden, and Mr. McKinstry, with the poet Thomas Campbell, had the good fortune to be near the scene of the combat; a cannon ball

2

struck near the spot where they were standing, which rather discomposed the nerves of the poet. Mr. McKinstry had seen the article before. Campbell's immortal poem commemorates this most bloody passage of arms.

We will dispose of this branch of the family by a brief notice of descendants in the female line, all of whom married and left children.

III. PRISCILLA, the eldest daughter of Dr. McKinstry, married John Hazen, Sept. 2, 1787. Mr. Hazen was nephew of General Hazen of N. H., who served in the French war, and also with reputation in the war of the revolution ; he died without issue in New York, in 1802. The nephew, after his marriage, established himself on a large and valuable farm at the junction of the Oromucto River with the St. John, in New Brunswick, where he died. They had twelve children, as follows :

IV. [1] ELIZA, b. July 14, 1788 ; m. Samuel Kimball, Esq., of Concord, N. H.
[2] WILLIAM McKINSTRY, b. April 26, 1790.
[3] GEORGE LEONARD, and JOHN, twins, b. July 16, 1792.
[4] MARY ANN, b. June 1, 1796.
[5] JAMES, b. March 9, 1798.
[6] ROBERT, b. March 28, 1800.
[7] THOMAS, b. Jan. 4, 1802.
[8] SARAH, b. March 16, 1704.
[9] CHARLOTTE, b. April 26, 1806.
[10] NATHANIEL MERRILL, b. April 24, 1808.

Mr. Hazen and his wife both died in New Brunswick.

III. SARAH, the 2d daughter of Dr. McKinstry,[2] married Major Caleb Stark, in Haverhill, in 1787. Major Stark was the eldest son of Gen. John Stark, of revolutionary fame, and was born Dec. 3, 1759. He accompanied his father as a volunteer, and was present at the battle of Bunker Hill ; soon after was appointed ensign in Capt. George Reid's company, in the 1st N. H. Regiment. He served in New York and Canada ; he was an adjutant in the battles of Trenton and Princeton ; was present at the battle of Saratoga, and Springfield, N. J. ; served as adjutant general of the Northern Department, in 1778 and 1781, and continued in service to the close of the war. After the peace he engaged in mercantile pursuits ; was awhile established in Boston with his brother-in-law, John McKinstry, and engaged in manufacturing at Pembroke, N. H. He was a man of great courage, energy, and perseverance through life. He died in Ohio, August 26, 1838, where he had proceeded to establish a claim to land granted for military services. The principal residence of his family was a fine seat in Dunbarton, N. H., which still belongs to the family, and is their summer resort.

Mrs. Stark died Sept. 11, 1839, aged 72. Their children were :

IV. [1] JOHN WILLIAM, d. Jan. 6, 1836, without issue.

    [2] HARRIET and SARAH, twins. Sarah d. in infancy. Harriet is living.

    [3] ELIZABETH, m. Samuel Newell of Boston, and is living.

    [4] CHARLES and SARAH, twins, both dead. Charles unmarried. Sarah married Joshua Winslow.

    [5] HENRY, married and living.   [7] CHARLOTTE, living unmarried.

    [6] MARY ANNE, died unmarried.   [8] CALEB, living unmarried.

    [9] DAVID McKINSTRY, died unmarried, Oct. 26, 1832.

Of these, Harriet, Elizabeth, Charlotte, Henry and Caleb are surviving. (1858.). Harriet, Charlotte and Caleb, unmarried. Elizabeth married Samuel Newell, and has one son surviving. Sarah married Joshua Winslow of Boston, both dead, leaving one son, a lieutenant in the navy. Caleb is a graduate of H. C., 1823, and by profession a lawyer, but has given his principal attention to literary and historical studies. He has published a life of his grandfather, the celebrated General, and memoirs of his father and other members of the family. I am indebted to him for many interesting facts contained in this notice.

III. MARY, the third daughter of Dr. McKinstry,[2] married Benjamin Willis, January 9, 1791. He was the eldest son of Benjamin Willis, who was born in Boston, 1743, only son of Benjamin Willis, of that town, who died in 1745. Mr. Willis, born in Charlestown, March, 1768, then lived in Haverhill, to which place his family had fled from the flames of Charlestown, where they then resided, June 17, 1775. He moved to Portland, Me., in 1803, and to Boston in 1815. His wife died in Boston, Feb. 12, 1847, after a union of fifty-six years; he died Oct. 1, 1853, aged 85 years and over 7 months. They had eight children, viz:

IV. [1] BENJAMIN, born at Haverhill, Nov. 16, 1791.

    [2] WILLIAM,   "   "   "   Aug. 31, 1794.

    [3] GEORGE,   "   "   "   June 16, 1797, d. Oct. 24, 1844.

    [4] THOMAS,   "   "   "   March 15, 1800, d. July, 1814, unm.

    [5] HENRY,   "   "   "   April 13, 1802.

    [6] MARY,   "   " Portland, Dec. 14, 1805.

    [7] ELIZABETH, "   "   "   Oct. 25, 1807, d. May 3, 1856.

    [8] THOMAS LEONARD, b. at Portland, April 4, 1812, d. Sept. 13, 1845.

IV. BENJAMIN,[1] married Elizabeth Sewall, daughter of Col. Joseph May of Boston, Sept. 19, 1817. She died in 1822, leaving two children, Hamilton and Elizabeth. The latter married Thomas G. Wells, and with her father and family is now living at Walpole, N. H. Hamilton married Louisa Winship and lives in Boston. He was a successful merchant in Portland, until he retired from business on a competency.

IV. WILLIAM,[2] graduated at Harvard College in 1813 ; was admitted to the Suffolk Bar in 1817 ; moved to Portland in 1819, where he is still in the practice of his profession. He married, in 1823, Relia, a daughter of the Hon. Ezekiel Whitman, late Chief Justice of the Supreme Court of Maine, by whom he has had eight children, all of whom died unmarried, except Julia, born 1829; married to Dr. Barron C. Watson, in 1852, and now resident in New York ; and Henry, born June 5, 1831, married to Adeline Fitch, 1855, and is living in Portland, in the practice of law. Each has one child, (1858.)

IV. GEORGE,[3] late a merchant in Portland, Me. ; married, 1st, Caroline, daughter of Col. Richard Hunnewell, by whom he had one child, which died in infancy. 2d, Clarissa May, daughter of Caleb Hall, Esq., by whom he had nine children ; three sons, George H., Benjamin W., and Caleb Hall, with five daughters, survive. He died Oct. 24, 1844. His sons are unmarried ; four daughters are married and have issue.

IV. HENRY,[4] a merchant ; resides in Roxbury, Mass., unmarried. He represents that city in the Legislature in 1858.

IV. MARY,[5] married the Hon. James H. Duncan of Haverhill, Mass., June 28, 1826. He is a graduate of H. C., 1812. By him she has had thirteen children, of whom nine are living, viz., three sons—James H., a graduate of Brown Univer. ; Samuel W., now a member of that institution, and George W. None of the children are married but Mary W., who was married to Mr. Harris of Illinois, in 1857. Mr. Duncan was born in Haverhill, Dec. 5, 1793, son of James Duncan, a descendant of the Scotch-Irish stock of Londonderry. He has twice represented his District in Congress, been a member of the Council, and held other important offices.

IV. ELIZABETH,[7] married the Hon. Henry W. Kinsman of Newburyport, son of Dr. Aaron Kinsman of Portland and Ann Willis, sister of Benjamin, Oct. 1, 1828. He was born in Portland, 1803 ; graduated at Dartmouth College, and was connected in law business with Daniel Webster, in Boston, prior to his moving to Newburyport. He has represented his State in the Senate and House of Representatives of Massachusetts. By his wife he had eleven children, all unmarried ; three daughters only survive. His wife died May 6, 1856, aged 49. *Oc*

IV. THOMAS LEONARD,[3] a merchant, afterwards farmer in Illinois ; married Charlotte Elizabeth, daughter of Caleb Hall, Esq., of Bucksport, Oct. 11, 1832. They had six children, three only survive, two daughters and one son, Thomas L. One daughter, Ellen, in 1857, married Joseph A. Ware of Portland, now of Chicago, Ill. He died Sept. 13, 1845, aged 33.

III. ELIZABETH, the fourth and youngest daughter of Dr. William McKinstry,[2] born Oct. 26, 1772, was married to Samuel Sparhawk of Portsmouth, in 1803. Mr. Sparhawk was a man of fine family, was connected with the Hon. Nathaniel Sparhawk of New Hampshire, and himself held many offices in his native State, of honor and trust. He was several years Secretary of State, and a man of unimpeachable integrity and honor. They had but three children.

    IV. [1] OLIVER, married, and died without issue.

      [2] THOMAS.

      [3] ELIZABETH, married Edward Winslow, son of Isaac Winslow of Boston, and has no children.

    IV. THOMAS resides in Amesbury, Mass.; married a Scotch lady and has children. He is a physician, skilful and in good practice.

II. PAUL, the fifth child and youngest son of the Rev. John[1] of Ellington, born Sept. 18, 1734, died March 14, 1818. He had three wives. By the 1st, Sarah Laird of Stafford, Conn., he had five children born in Ellington, viz: ALEXANDER,[1] SALMON,[2] ALVIN,[3] ELIZABETH,[4] ALICE.[5] By his second wife he had two children, SARAH,[6] and WILLIAM,[7] who were born in Bethel, Vermont, to which place their parents had moved. By his 3d wife he had no children. His first wife died Aug. 5, 1778, aged 36.

    III. [1] ALEXANDER, his eldest son, was born Dec. 12, 1764, and died in Vermont, Feb. 15, 1817. He had seven children, one son and six daughters. His son, Alexander,[4] is living in Syracuse, N. Y., in 1858; he has three sons and one daughter.

    III. [2] Salmon, b. Oct. 2, 1766; married and had a family in Stafford, Conn., of five sons and seven daughters.

    III. [3] ALVIN, b. July 3, 1769; died Oct. 3, 1853; left one son, Paul, and one daughter, Emily. Paul is living (1857) in Newbury, Vt., and has had eight children, viz.: three sons and five daughters; six are living.

    III. [4] ELIZABETH, b. Nov. 28, 1771; married —— Loomis, and had a large family.

    III. [5] ALICE, b. Aug. 17, 1774; married Othniel Eddy of Vermont, and had nine children.

    III. [6] SARAH, b. 1783; married Joel Eddy, brother of Othniel, and had nine children, seven sons and two daughters. Six living in 1857.

    III. [7] WILLIAM, b. May 19, 1784. He is living ~~a bachelor and~~ a respectable and wealthy merchant, in Middletown, Conn., 1858. He has recently erected a handsome monument to his grandparents, the Rev. John McKinstry[1] and wife, over their remains, in the ancient burying ground in Ellington, with suitable inscriptions.

Another branch of the McKinstry family came to this country. Tradition and circumstances furnish strong evidence of a common origin with the branch I have been describing, and I conjecture that they descended either from a brother or son of Rodger. The first comer of this family was—

I. Capt. JOHN McKINSTRY, who was born in Armagh, in the Province of Ulster, Ireland, in 1712. He married Jane Dickie, widow of —————— Belknap, of the County of Antrim. He came to this country about 1740 ; remained near Boston, awhile, then went to Londonderry, in New Hampshire, where his first son, JOHN, was born, 1745. His other children were, Thomas, David, Charles and Sarah. Sarah, b. 1754 ; married Dr. Bird, of Hinsdale, N. Y., and had two daughters, Nancy and Hannah. She died in 1780, aged 26. Mrs. McKinstry (Belknap) had one son by her first husband, who was an officer in the British army, and was in the service at New York, at the time of the revolution. A meeting was concerted between him and his brother-in-law, John McKinstry, about the time the British were evacuating New York, but it failed by the fleet's sailing before his brother reached the place of appointment. They were officers in the opposing forces. Capt. McKinstry was also an officer in the English army ; he died at Hinsdale, in N. Y., Oct. 6, 1776, aged 64.

II. JOHN, son of Capt. John,[1] b. 1745 ; married Elizabeth Knox of Rumford, Conn., by whom he had eight sons and three daughters, viz.:

[1] JAMES, b. in Blandford, Mass., May 2, 1767 ; d. April 1, 1768.
[2] RACHEL, b. March 16, 1769 ; married Sturgeon Sloan, an American officer, and died without issue, May 16, 1855.
[3] GEORGE, b. at Hinsdale, Jan. 20, 1772 ; living with a family, in Hudson, 1858.
[4] ELIZABETH, b. at Hinsdale, Nov. 24, 1774 ; married Walter T. Livingston and had issue.
[5] JOHN, b. at Hinsdale, Aug. 5, 1777 ; married and had issue.
[6] WILLIAM, b. at Hinsdale, Dec. 25, 1779 ; married and had issue.
[7] HENRY, b. at Hinsdale, Oct. 10, 1782 ; married and living in Hudson.
[8] SARAH, b. at Hudson, April 5, 1785 ; died Oct. 31, 1786.
[9] ANSEL, b. at Hudson, Sept. 30, 1787 ; living at Hudson, 1858.
[10] NATHANIEL GREEN, b. at Hinsdale, April 23, 1791 ; d. Sept. 4, 1794.
[11] ROBERT, b. at Livingston, Oct. 9, 1794 ; living at Hudson, 1858.

John, II., saw some service in the French war, though young ; and at the commencement of the revolution joined the American army ; was at the battle of Bunker Hill and the principal northern battles. He was taken prisoner at " the Cedars," in Canada, and came near losing his life to gratify savage revenge. He was bound to a stake and the faggots piled around him ; when, it occurring to him that the Indian chief, Brandt, was a mason, he communicated to him the masonic sign, which caused his immediate release and subsequent good treatment. He was afterwards promoted to a colonelcy in a New York regiment, and served during the war. He died at Livingston, June 9, 1822 ; his widow, April 7, 1833.

II. THOMAS, son of Capt. John,[1] married, 1st, Elizabeth Green, by whom he had Nancy and Thomas. By his 2d wife, he had Sarah, 1782, died 1851; Hollis died in Michigan, unmarried, 1858, and Orenzo. Hollis was the last surviving member of this family.

II. DAVID, son of John,[1] married Martha Cauley, by whom he had two sons, Charles and David ; and four daughters, Mary, Susan, Clarissa and Sarah.

II. CHARLES, son of John,[1] born at Blandford, 1755 ; mar. Tabitha Patterson, at Hinsdale, where he was living in 1774 ; she died, 1787, aged 32. In 1790, he married Nancy Norton of Farmington, who died May 24, 1798, aged 35. He died at Hinsdale, Dec. 31, 1819, aged 64. By his 1st wife, he had—

[1] JANE, married Asahel Porter, 1796, and had one son, Thomas, born 1798. They all died in Greenfield, N. Y.

[2] DAVID CHARLES, b. August 12, 1778 ; married and died at Ypsilanti, in Michigan, Sept. 9, 1856, leaving issue.

[3] SALLY, b. Aug 13, 1780 ; died at Hinsdale, April 17, 1845 ; married Augustus Tremain, 1798, and had issue, Charles Patterson, d. 1834, Augustus Porter, and Jane.

[4] OLIVE, b. June 9, 1783 ; d. 1788.

[5] JUSTUS, b. Oct. 27, 1785 ; died at the Astor House, N. Y., May 21, 1849.   [6] Daughter, died at birth, 1787.

By second wife, Nancy Norton, he had—

[7] CHARLES NORTON, b. Jan. 16, 1792 ; d. at Hinsdale, 1794.

[8] MELINDA, b. June 12, 1794 ; married Henry Loop of Hempstead, L. I., 1829, and has one son, Charles Norton Loop, a merchant in New York. She is the only survivor of the children, and is living in Hempstead, 1858.

[9] NANCY, b. July 28, 1796 ; married Bowen Whiting, Sept. 18, 1819, by whom she had one son, John Nicols, b. at Geneva, 1821, and is a lawyer in New York. She died at Geneva, July 24, 1847, and husband, at the same place, Dec. 1849.

[10] MARIANNE, b. May 16, 1798 ; d. May 24, 1798.

His 3d wife, whom he married at Great Barrington, Jan. 18, 1803, was Bernice Egliston, who died April 2, 1845, aged 76—by her,

[11] EDWARD WHITING, b. June 24, 1804 ; d. April 9, 1805.

[12] EDWIN, b. Nov. 10, 1805 ; died at Metamoras, March 9, 1849.

I add to what I have said above of the children of Charles, the son of John (1), the following particulars.

III. DAVID CHARLES, his 2d child, married Nancy Whiting Backus, 1805, who is now living at Ypsilanti; their children were—

[1] JAMES PATERSON, b. at Hinsdale, 1807, commander in U. S. N. ; married Jan. 23, 1858, Mary W. Smart, daughter of the late Gen. J. R. Williams of Detroit.

[2] SARAH INGERSOLL, b. 1809 ; living in Ypsilanti.

[3] AUGUSTUS TREMAIN, b. 1811 ; living at Ypsilanti.

[4] JUSTUS, b. at Hudson, 1814 ; grad. at West Point, 1838; married Susan McKinstry, daughter of George McKinstry (III.), 1838, and has three sons living—Charles Frederick, James H., and Carlisle P. He is a major in the U. S. Army.

[5] ANN, b. at Detroit, 1817 ; married Houston Van Clive, 1849, and has one daughter, Margaretta, and is living at Ann Arbor, Mich.

[6] CHARLES, b. at Detroit, 1819 ; graduated at New Brunswick, 1843, and was a lawyer in New York ; died June 23, 1855.

[7] ELISHA WILLIAMS, b. at Detroit, 1824. Judge of Supreme Court in California.

III.   GEORGE, 3d child of Col. John,[2] b. 1772 ; married Susan Hamilton, daughter of Patrick Hamilton, M. D., of Canaan, N. Y., and is now living in Hudson, N. Y. Their children were—

[1] ELIZA, b. in Canaan, Aug. 17, 1802 ; d. Feb. 1, 1804.

[2] ALEXANDER H., b. in Athens, N. Y., Feb. 17, 1805 ; mar. Angelina Pease and had five children, viz. : [1] Elisha, b. 1832, d. at St. Fe; [2] George B., b. 1834 ; [3] Oliver W., b. 1837 ; [4] Nora and Kathlene, died in infancy ; [5] Charles A., 1844. The mother is living at St. Louis with her children.

[3] JANE P., b. in Hudson, Nov. 21, 1808 ; living in Hudson.

[4] GEORGE, b. in Hudson, Sept. 15, 1810 ; living in California.

[5] JAMES, b. in Hudson, Dec. 25, 1812 ; d. in infancy.

[6] SUSAN, b. in Hudson, June 1, 1814 ; married her kinsman, James P. McKinstry, son of David Charles (II.), a major in the U. S. A., stationed in Florida, and had five children, viz. : Angelica and Susan H., both d. in infancy ; [3] Charles F., b. 1843 ; [4] James H., b. 1845 ; [5] Carlisle, b. 1854.

[7] CHARLES, b. in Hudson, Sept. 17, 1816 ; d. at Perry, Mo., April 14, 1841. He married Ellen H. Avery, and had one daughter, Cassandra, b. at Claverack, N. Y., 1840, and d. 1845. His widow married his brother, Augustus.

[8] JOHN, b. at Hudson, Sept 9, 1818 ; d. Jan. 3, 1824.

[9] AUGUSTUS, b. at Hudson, Dec. 5, 1821 ; is living at Hudson, 1858. He married his brother Charles's widow, and has two children : Jeannie, b. Nov. 5, 1851, and George A., b. Feb. 20, 1855.

III. ELIZABETH, dau. of Col. John,[2] b. 1774; d. 1841; married Walter T. Livingston of Livingston, N. Y., and had five children, viz.:

[1] WILLIAM R., b. May 1, 1799.
[2] SUSAN M., b. June 12, 1802; d. Aug. 20, 1805.
[3] JANE, b. Sept. 4, 1804; married Hon. John Sanders of Schenectady, and had three children, Walter T., Eugene L., and Mary E.
[4] MARY T., b. May 20, 1810; d. Dec. 11, 1838.
[5] SUSAN, b. May 4, 1816; married Peter Van Deusen of Greenport, L. I., and had Mary L., Anna, Jeannie, Livingston, and one died.
   The mother, Elizabeth, is living at Greenport, 1858.

III. JOHN, son of Capt. John,[2] b. 1777; married 1st, Elizabeth Smith, and had—

[1] MARY ANN.
[2] WILLIAM H., married 1st, Elizabeth Gavett, by whom he had one child, who died in infancy. By 2d wife he had four children,— Edwin, Charles, Mary and John, living in Greenport.
[3] ELIZA, married George Decker of Greenport, and had Jacob, living in New York; Robert, dead; Helen living at Greenport with parents.
[4] RACHEL, married Dr. Charles H. Skiff of New Haven, and had two children, viz.: Elizabeth died an infant, and Charles, living with parents in New Haven.
[5] ROBERT.
   By 2d wife, Salome Root, he had—
[6] JOHN,
[7] SLOAN, } both living in Dixon, Ill., with whom their mother is living.
   The father died Sept. 30, 1846.

III. WILLIAM, son of Col. John,[2] b. Dec. 25, 1779, d. Dec. 2, 1829; married Rebecca Barnard, and had DANIEL P. and WILLIAM C., who died at sea. William C. married Amelia Luddington, and had four children. ELIZA, 3d child of William, married Walter B. Crane, and has two children, living with her at Rondout, N. Y.

III. HENRY, son of Col. John,[2] b. 1782; married Julia Day, widow of Capt Gardiner, by whom he had six children, viz.:

[1] HENRY, b. June 29, 1808; d. 1809.
[2] PHILO, b. March 14, 1810; d. 1810.
[3] HELEN, b. April 17, 1811; d. 1847, at Greenport. She mar. William Griggs of Greenport, and had one son, now living in New York.
[4] DELIA, b. Sept. 1, 1813; d. 1815 at Catskill.
[5] EDWARD H., b. Aug. 21, 1815; d. 1836 at Catskill.
[6] SHERWOOD, b. Aug. 4, 1823; d. 1823 at Catskill.
   He is living at Hudson, having survived all his children.

III. ANSEL, son of Col. John,[2] b. 1787; living at Hudson, 1858. He married, 1st, Sarah McKinstry, and had—[1] ELIZABETH, b. 1817, d. young; a [2] SON, died an infant; and [3] DELIA, b. 1821, d. 1833. By his 2d wife, Caroline Bemis, he has no issue.

III. ROBERT, son of Col. John,[2] b. 1774; married Sally Hammond and has no issue; is now living at Hudson.

I find a third and distinct branch of the McKinstry family, which came to this country at a different time from either of the other two. They, as well as the others, went from the vicinity of Edinburgh to Ireland. The grandfather and father of WILLIAM, the first of this branch who came to this country, emigrated from Scotland to Carrickfergus in Ireland, prior to 1700.

I. WILLIAM, born in Carrickfergus in 1722; immigrated to this country in 1740 or '41, and landed in Boston. He went first to Medfield, where he remained about seven years. He then established himself in that part of Sturbridge which is now Southbridge, Mass., in 1748, on a farm, which has ever since been occupied by his descendants, in a direct line, to the present day. In 1751 he married Mary Morse, by whom he had thirteen children, viz. :

II. [1] JAMES, married and had thirteen children, as hereinafter stated.

[2] SARAH, married and died in New York in 1814.

[3] WILLIAM, married Esther Robbins, and had a family, as hereafter stated.

[4] MOLLY, married Ephraim Bacon, and died without issue, 1828.

[5] AMOS, was a soldier in the army of the revolution. He moved to Vermont, where he died in 1844, leaving a family. His sons are all dead.

[6] JOHN, also a soldier in the army; married and moved to the neighborhood of Seneca Falls, in New York, where he died, leaving a family. Two of his sons only living. One, Horace H., in Stillwater, Minnesota, the other in Michigan.

[7] EXPERIENCE, married and moved to Vermont, where she died, leaving issue.

[8] ELIZABETH, married William Saunders, and died in Charlton, 1852.

[9] JOSEPH, died in Sturbridge, 1809, unmarried.

[10] MARGARET, died in Connecticut, 1822.

[11] ALEXANDER, died in infancy.

[12] JANE, died in Sturbridge, 1793, unmarried.

[13] NATHAN, a distinguished physician and surgeon, died in Newbury, Vt., unmarried, in 1815.

II. JAMES, the eldest son of William (I.), married Lois Dix in 1773, and died in Southbridge. By her he had thirteen children, viz. :

III.   ¹ JAMES.   ⁸ NANCY.
       ² ALEXANDER.   ⁹ DAVID, died in 1857.
       ³ ANNA.   ¹⁰ DANIEL.
       ⁴ LOIS.   ¹¹ MARTHA.
       ⁵ MARY.   ¹² MOSES, died young.
       ⁶ WILLIAM.   ¹³ MOSES.
       ⁷ BENJAMIN, died in 1857.

Descendants of the foregoing children of James (II.) are numerous and much scattered over the country.   I regret that I have not the means of giving a more extended account of them.

II.   WILLIAM, 3d son of William (I.) married Esther Robbins in 1785, and had children as follows, viz. :

III .¹ JOHN, born in 1786.   ⁴ WILLIAM.
     ² ELIZABETH.   ⁵ SILAS, died in 1856.
     ³ MARY.

III.   JOHN, son of William (II.) is now living at Southbridge, and is the father of John O., Esq. a member of the House of Representatives of Massachusetts, in 1858, from Southbridge.   He was born in 1786 ; married Kezia Batcheller of Charlton, born 1787, and lives on the homestead, which has been in the family 110 years.   His seven children were—

IV.   ¹ MARY, died in infancy.
      ² PREVOSTERS, married twice.   By his first wife he had
            V.   ¹ JOHN H.,who lives in Brighton, Iowa.
                 ² ELLIOT F., who lives with his father in Southbridge.
            By his 2d wife he has one son and three daughters, all minors.
      ³ WILLIAM F., son of John (III.) is married and has three daughters ; Mary, Elizabeth, and Alice.
      ⁴ MANILLEE, married Verney Fiske, and has had nine children ; one daughter and two sons dead ; five sons and one daughter living.   The eldest son, John D. Fiske, was married in 1857, and lives in Chelsea, Mass.
      ⁵ ELIZA, married Adam Miller, who died in 1849, leaving two children, Frank and Anna.   She remains a widow.
      ⁶ A daughter, married Adolphus Merriam, by whom she has had one daughter, Lucy, and two sons, Joseph and an infant,
      ⁷ JOHN O., married Elizabeth R. Spaulding, born in Thompson, Ct., and have had five children ; Charles O. and George F., deceased ; John Willard, Eliza and Ira Jacobs—the eldest nine years old.

III.   WILLIAM, 4th child of William 2d, married Matilda Marcy, by whom he has had—
IV.   ¹ ESTHER, married to Aretas Hooker ; she died several years since, leaving one son and one daughter.

[2] ELIJAH, unmarried.

[3] NATHAN, married Hannah Taylor, by whom he had five children, of whom four are living, viz. : Mary, Lemuel, George B., and Jude.

[4] WILLIAM, married Mary Ann Kitchen, by whom he has two children, Cassius and Charlotte.

[5] JOHN A., unmarried.

[6] MARY, married George Brackett ; live in Sturbridge ; no children. He is still living.

III. SILAS, 5th child of William McKinstry (II.), married Lucy Twiss, by whom he has had two children, who have died, and the following, who survive. ALBERT, JAMES T., CHARLES and ASA, living in Southbridge, and HENRY in Kanzas, all unmarried. Silas died in 1856.

III. ELIZABETH, 2d child and eldest daughter of William (II.) married Asa Dresser, by whom she had seven children ; only one, SYLVESTER, is living. SILAS, another son, married and left seven children, all living except one. Their only daughter married and left one son, Julius Knowlton. Elizabeth is living.

III. MARY, 2d daughter and 3d child of William (II.), married Luther Clemence, by whom she had six children, all living, viz. : [1] HARRY, married and has two children. [2] FIDELIA, unmarried. [3] JOHN McK., married and has one son living, one dead. [4] MERCY, married Washington White of Charlton, and has one child living and unmarried. Mary is still living.

My account of this family is very imperfect. I did not know of its existence until last winter, and did not receive the minutes I now publish until the preceding part of my manuscript had gone to press. The numerous members of this branch, from what I believe to be a common stock, springing from the midlands of Scotland, and now contributing by their industry, intelligence and skill, to build up the towns and waste places of our western world, had their primal seat in this country, at Southbridge, where many of the elder race remain to preserve and perpetuate the sound principles they inherited from their virtuous ancestors. I hope this imperfect notice will incite them or some of them to collect and transmit full details of all branches of this respected and honorable family.